TAILS
OF FRIENDSHIP:

GROWING UP WITH MY FIRST PETS

WHISKERS, WAGGING, TAILS AND WONDERFUL MEMORIES AWAIT!

BY ASHLEY JONES

DEDICATION

This book is dedicated to all the children who find love, laughter, and endless adventures in the company of their beloved pets. May your hearts be forever warmed by the paw prints left on your journey through childhood.

ABOUT THE AUTHOR

Ashley is a passionate storyteller and animal lover who finds inspiration in the simple joys of everyday life. With a background in childhood education and a deep appreciation for the bond between humans and their pets, Ashley brings warmth and authenticity to her writing. Her stories aim to capture the magic of childhood and the special relationships that shape our lives. When she's not writing, Ashley enjoys spending time with her own furry friends, exploring nature, and discovering new adventures with her family.

ABOUT THE AUTHOR

Ashley is a passionate storyteller and animal lover who finds inspiration in the simple joys of everyday life. With a background in childhood education and a deep appreciation for the bond between humans and their pets, Ashley brings warmth and authenticity to her writing. Her stories aim to capture the magic of childhood and the special relationships that shape our lives. When she's not writing, Ashley enjoys spending time with her own furry friends, exploring nature, and discovering new adventures with her family.

Tiny but mighty,
Marley's ready to shine.
With her eyes so big,
she looks so bright.

First day at preschool,

Marley's excitement shows.

She cannot wait to come back

to gifts with shiny bows.

Marley meets Max and
Luna with sparkling eyes.
A cute dog and a cat,
such a delight!

Round and round,

they play in the sun.

Hide and seek, oh what fun!

Books and stories,
Marley loves to read,
Max and Luna cuddle;
that is all they need.

"It's moving day!" A new place for the friends to play and roam. Max and Luna are excited to get a new home.

Candles glowing, cake on a tray.
Max and Luna celebrate
Marley's birthday!

School is a bit hard, but
Marley is okay because
with Max and Luna,
her troubles go away.

High School days come
with studies and more.
Marley still finds time,
which her pets adore.

Caps in the air,
it's time to cheer.
It is finally Marley's
graduation year!

Among friends, time flies.
Under bright and sunny skies.

True friendship never ends. That is one thing we can learn from Marley and her friends.

The three of them together,
there is joy all around.
Their adventures continue
and their love knows no bound.

Made in the USA
Middletown, DE
24 August 2024

59657114R00018